Little Book of Days

NONA CASPERS

SPUYTEN DUYVIL

New York City

Nona Caspers is also the author of

Heavier Than Air: Stories
(University of Massachusetts Press)
Winner of the Grace Paley Prize in Short Fiction
Editors' Choice, New York Times Book Review

LITTLE BOOK OF DAYS

Author's Note and Acknowledgments

This book started as a project to track my days, which I did for four-hundred days. I am grateful for the literary conversation, editing, and friendship of poet Barbara Tomash (*Flying in Water, The Secret of White*). Jesse Nissim, Molly Albrecht, Sandi Kaplan, and Elaine Buckholtz also gave me helpful responses to the manuscript. Kai Lundgren supplied philosophical inspiration on dailiness. Toni Mirosevich encouraged me to continue. Judy Bloch proofread the manuscript. Sandi Kaplan and Jim Moe gave me permission to embody them with language, understanding the limited nature of point of view and perception.

I also am grateful for the financial support for this project from San Francisco State University. And finally, big thanks to Tod Thilleman and Spuyten Duyvil Press for making this book possible and for making the literary conversation more exciting.

Excerpts of an earlier version of this book appeared in the Sidebrow Litopolis project (sidebrow.net/2006/litopolissf.php) and in *Lesbian Harrington Fiction Quarterly* under the title "This My Life."

ISBN 978-1-933132-69-3

Library of Congress Cataloging-in-Publication Data

Caspers, Nona.
Little book of days / Nona Caspers.
p. cm.
ISBN 978-1-933132-69-3
1. Experimental fiction. I. Title.
PS3553.A79523L57 2009
813'.54--dc22
2008050093

For Elaine Buckholtz

Every day the glory is ready to emerge from its debasement.
—Rabbi Nachman of Bratslav

Consciousness has no climax.

—Mina Loy

Prologue

THE RADIO says arctic ground squirrels live underground for eight months a year. They lower their body temperature below freezing without freezing themselves, and they lie underground and no one expects anything of them. They are not asleep, they are frozen without being frozen.

Yesterday, after I did yoga, I lay on my back on the gray carpet breathing and it became clear to me that I had to carry my body through millions more minutes. How do I explain this? There is no pause button.

I am beginning to believe we are all going to die.

The squirrels have to be pure when they lower their temperature, the radio says, because if crystallization starts, even one microscopic icicle formed around a body salt, they freeze from the inside out. When they wake up, everyone wants to eat them.

GONE. In bed thinking about T, who is long gone, and then thinking about V, who is just gone, and then waiting for something to happen. "The light gleams an instant," says Beckett. I am terrified that nothing will happen and terrified that something will happen and I can feel the molecules of my body careening in time.

A blue car drives by on 15th Street.

I suppose I should get out of bed, but the weight of my body seems enormous. As soon as I get out of bed I am responsible for everything I do or don't do. I wish someone would invade my body; I envy those people in B movies who become possessed—it would be such a relief from this human condition. The garbage truck clanks to a stop in front of the apartment building.

THE WORD *demise* keeps coming up on the radio and then on Muni. The demise of the Roman Empire, the demise of the global climate as we know it. The demise of small neighborhood stores. The demise of family-owned farms. The demise of hardcover books. The demise of Alaskan shorelines (along with common decency). The demise of one-piece bathing suits. The demise of Angelina and Brad Pitt's relationship. Who are they? The East Indian man in the front seat asks.

TREPIDATION. I wake up in a panic. I can't remember my worth. I want V, but of course V is not for me. I pace between the couch and red writing table in my living room and wish for the tenth time this morning that I could have Jesus. Why does everyone (the woman on the radio) get to have Jesus but me? If I had Jesus he would carry me through these mornings, hoist me up or maybe he'd hang me over his shoulder, like Rock Hudson with Doris Day. If I had Jesus I would drop to my knees.

I guess I could drop to my knees anyway.

I drop to my knees in front of the stack of unread *New Yorkers* on the coffee table.

Green trees up against gray sky, the air full of rain.

Sheets of rain slick up 15th Street. On the phone D talks about Sylvia Plath and we disagree about the structure of emotions. Is anger primary or secondary? And what about trepidation?

I THINK despair should be reserved for natural disasters; death of children, pets, parents, and siblings; assault; war; rape; horrible wounds. In the middle of listening to someone, X, telling me a sad story about her life I start fantasizing that my mother, who is happily square dancing in Minnesota, has suicided, that I am telling a roomful of people about how much I love my mother and then I start to cry, real time, not in the fantasy. Tears creep up in my eyes and X makes a face like *Oh, Nona, she's so compassionate.*

My neighbor is stomping above me.

Then I have this Old Testament–like instinct in my gut or maybe in a bone to make sure god knows I don't want my mother to die, and I think about the likelihood of that—she would never take such *action.* And then I imagine myself telling people *I'm almost proud of her; she was always so passive.*

Later, when I'm on the couch watching someone have heart surgery on the medical channel, I imagine it's my baby brother who dies, and then I tell people *he's the one I helped raise.*

SHINE. The wild, renegade parrots are squawking in the palm trees on Dolores, and on 15th Street a young man breaks into ballsy gospel at the top of his lungs. He flings his arms into the air.

High of sixty-one degrees with cloudy skies, westerly winds, or maybe he said easterly, at fifteen miles per hour, morning fog, and a chance of sunshine later in the day. (Norm Howard, the announcer, has a cold.)

SEVEN THIRTY A.M. Sunday. I open my eyes to the Virgin Mary's green eyes and heavy-hooded lids. Her flames of compassion. I force myself to lie in bed and try to become curious about the day, though what I really want is to go underground until spring's golden yarrow, calla lilies, lunaria, monarchs. A red car drives by on 15th Street.

After T left so suddenly (the moment she told me she was leaving it was as if I always knew), I taped a postcard picturing a million sunflowers to my kitchen wall, but in a week I had to tear the card down. All those possibilities waving and waving in the wind.

I left V (knew that would happen too).

They say there is no wrong choice but we all know they are wrong.

"The light gleams an instant, then it's night once more."

The squirrels live in Alaska. Canada in the Yukon. Alpine and arctic tundra meadows. Riverbanks. Lakeshores. Sandbanks.

If I could wake up like a normal person I would. (Who is honking so loudly?) But when I first gain consciousness these days, I have to work my way out of the grave through the panic of structureless void to reach those damn sunflowers.

The garbage truck clanks to a stop in front of the building.

The longer I lie in bed the scarier it gets so I leap out. *Thank you Mother Mary.*

I stand in front of the bedroom windows and lift my hands above my head. I drop from the waist and let my breath dangle over that grave.

LANGUAGE is a box you wear over your head. You listen for traffic in the dream like you listen for company, anticipation a wheel and a heart thumping—now bright sun and silence, a slipping sound. A girl jumps from chair to chair, her bare feet flying out in front of her and a suspension—these people pass through our lives, their faces are the surface of the moon, a very tender gray eye: *Here we are, together again.* Wordless and watery and whalelike.

RAIN. The red dirt mixes with the blue sky making trees and air violet. Walls will not talk but lend themselves to a winter view. I hang up the phone and sit at the red table in front of the bay windows. Instead of going *Oh, there goes another nasty thought!* I throw a pen at my foot. I find a cord of white string in a drawer I never open and tie the pen to the track light on the living room ceiling. Track lighting was invented in the 1960s in Fall River, Massachusetts, by the Lightolier Company. *Track lighting is ideal for adding focused illumination to particular areas.* The kittens toss the pen into space and watch it swing. It knocks Fido in the head and she leaps back, surprised, exhilarated. Goes after it as if it were alive.

10 p.m. The radio says 164,000 people have died today. Of we who left the house, 1.5 million walked through Times Square. I sit on the couch, streaks of gray and white, and then down comes the scene where T drives away in her blue Horizon. It's raining out—that's what keeps me from joining the masses of people going out to rent a movie.

MY NEIGHBOR comes out of his studio cocoon across the hall. We never talk, because he is inside himself packed in gel. Sometimes on my walk to work down Market Street I walk behind him and watch his legs turn out as he walks. The faded tape on his mailbox says his name is Andrew. Once I tried to send him a touch like in the German movie *Wings of Desire* when Peter Falk touches those in despair. I stared at Andrew's small back and narrow hips and concentrated. This could be extreme arrogance.

These are my kittens, I say. I introduce him to Spot who has no spots and Fido who looks nothing like a Fido, and he bends down and wiggles his fingers.

Hello, he says.   Hello.   Kitty.   Kitty.

Spot and Fido back off and puff and spit. Andrew's fingers begin to look ridiculous in the air so I throw their mouse out into the hall and they forget about dissing Andrew. I start to babble about how I'm trying to increase their territory and Andrew backs off into his apartment.

DURING THE NIGHT I forget what's true about my essential self. There is an anti-Hegelian hole under my queen-size bed where the truth leaks out.

D says maybe you're trying too hard.

A woman left her car parking lights on.

Everyone's turning left on Dolores Street today. Blink, blink, blink.

The day is gray, which says nothing about the weather. A white truck pulls up, red car whizzes by, another white truck, a meter maid truck looks like a toy truck, Office Depot truck, construction truck, M&M airport shuttle van, BART shuttle, green business truck, four-door Ford, brown sports convertible, a lull, rain, a white van, jeep, van, lull.

A woman is wearing a beige hat. She is looking down at the hem of her coat, her hands deep in her pockets.

BONES. 10 a.m. What am I after? Story seems like every other story. The pain might be interesting, but that's not what I'm after, really. People in the street are whistling—and for each other! Bubbie! he shouts. My Bubbie!, now in great despair, his Safeway cart rolling and clanking down 15th Street.

The meditation tape says put a blue ball of light in my right hand and a red ball of light in my left. Desire and longing in one hand and thwart in the other. I lift the balls over my head until they're one white ball and then I rest that on the back of my neck.

11 a.m. Vertical goals:

1. write a best-selling mystery novel and then buy a house with a green lawn
2. find inner peace
3. buy a living room rug
4. at least fix my freezer door and get my windows clean.

A list is the bones of plot the way desire is the bones of character.

I go into the bathroom and look under the tub at the kittens. I pet them. I should feed them. I give them a handful of Science Diet as recommended by vets. They gobble it up crunching while I pee and then they run back under the tub. I lie on the bathroom floor and tell them about all the toys I'm going to buy for them and how sorry I am that they can't go outside. The skinny one walks across my face to get to the water bowl. She stares at me. She drapes herself over my neck. Life! Life!

SOUP. Went to lunch with G and A and H. Pad Thai noodles. Green booths. Next to me, G sat before a bowl of udon noodle soup. She was sad because her girlfriend doesn't want to commit to any Thanksgiving plans. She offered me soup, moved her bowl toward me and I kept gesturing not yet not yet and later she asked again—soup? soup? and I waved my hand and finally she picked up her bowl and deliberately moved it back in front of her with a harrumph and ate it all.

Oh, I didn't get that you were waiting, I said.

Yes, she said. I was waiting.

What's this shame?

Arctic ground squirrels dream. Scientists know this. They wake up because they dream. What do they dream about? Topsoil? Sun? Arctic wolves galloping toward them?

Despite continuous summer light, arctic ground squirrels are active between four in the afternoon and nine or ten at night. On sunny days they forage and occasionally pause to sunbathe, sand-bathe, or swim; on rainy and cloudy days, they reside in their tunnel-connected burrows about three feet under the ground.

Seeds, berries, bog rush fruit, willow leaves, mushrooms, fungi, roots of grasses, sedges, flowers.

Apple, bread, yogurt, carrots, peas, mayonnaise.

Grizzly bears dig up whole systems of burrows to feast on the squirrels.

Arctic ground squirrels are very vocal, and because of the sounds they make, the Inupiat Eskimos in Alaska call them "sik-sik."

"Sik-sik." Sik-sik. What would someone name me?

GONE. Even though V is gone, I picture her with a cigarette in her mouth, glaring at me. Why would I miss someone glaring?

One day V and I went to the aquarium in Monterey and stood before the glory of jellyfish, floating orange plasma, the water passing through the film. I want that kind of spaciousness, the wind blowing through my skin. Green.

But I also want nothing like that.

A Latina pushing a blue stroller, the baby sucking on a bottle, swinging her legs, being moved to the park. A man on a bicycle, pasty skinned, pedaling across the intersection ignoring the cars as if two tons of metal couldn't hurt him. Is that high self-esteem or low self-esteem?

The truth about romantic love is that it has little to do with peace or security. Security is illusion, everyone knows. Peace comes from inside. People change, people die. The people I hate will die and the people I love will die and the people I don't care about or know or think I'm better than or who think they're better than me will change and die.

J says god can take him anytime. This when we're in a truck tootling out to Marin for catered food and he won't put on his seat belt. But, I say, are you ready to live in a wheelchair as a quadriplegic for the rest of your life? Oh, he says. That.

I USED TO mix up Roy Rogers and Ronald Reagan. "We make up most of our history around here…codger." Said Rogers. When Reagan was running for president I kept thinking Roy Rogers was running, and I couldn't understand how he got to be a presidential candidate. I remember sitting in a broken recliner at Cole's house out in Newton Valley, Wisconsin, the wood stove cranking out heat—we could have worn bathing suits in the middle of winter—and Sparky drove up in his truck full of electrical wire and marijuana lathes and burst in and announced tearfully that Ronald Reagan had won. We'd all voted for some wild independent radical. Sparky sat on the piano bench, which was unaccompanied by piano, and wept and said this was bad enough but if George Bush ever got to be president he was moving to Panajachel.

That winter, while chopping and stacking wood, I kept picturing the president of the United States on a white horse, throwing a lasso. Like so much of my life, I just didn't understand the requirements.

Why am I still so confused about the living and the dead? And identities? Today Terry Gross is talking to Roy Rogers on the radio. But I don't think it's the horse guy, because he's dead, isn't he?

"When my time comes, just skin me and put me up there on Trigger, just as though nothing had ever changed."

MOVIE. Last night, during the French movie sitting next to S, I started fantasizing that I had been raped and badly injured, maybe knifed, maybe beaten.

Andrew is hauling something out of his room again.

The mechanism of injury was not the fantasy. The fantasy was post injury. I was in the hospital and people were visiting me: D and G and J and S. In the fantasy, my friends hovered over me and whispered to each other. (Maybe T will show up—S will surely tell T—is that what I want?)

Then I wrote about it, and this was in the fantasy too, I wrote: *This is the story I have to tell. I wish it weren't my story. I don't know how to tell this story. But this is the story inside me. And now it will be inside you.*

Andrew has closed his door.

S leaned into me and asked did I want some more popcorn, and then she put her hand on the back of my head and I could feel all her silver rings. The French man fell in love with his own fiction.

DEEP BLUE. Silver. Black. Cooing. Whoosh, whoosh. A ringing bell and then more black. Not without a long silence. Not without knowing the three bones of the inner ear. Incus, malleus, stapes. Flesh colored— who told her to wear that shirt?

I sit on two pillows in the middle of my bed and follow my breath, until a point in the middle of my neck hurts. It's as if my lungs are directly attached to that exact muscle. The meditation book says describe the pain, but all I see is this orange disc on the back of my eyelids. Now the disc blows out trillions of white specks.

Another red car honks—it seems as if the brighter cars are always the honkers. Blue sky. A tall thin man with a green backpack. What does he see, gawking like that? My white refrigerator?

The sky glazes over the color of ice.

LIGHT. Underneath the table. Outside the frame of the window. The space between the bottom of the cup and the plate. Where light meets darkness. The orange of my pants—would they look as orange on you? Pour six glasses of milk and compare that light to the moon.

WHITE. Based on the dinosaur's special hinged bird ankle and bird hip bone that points down and backwards, and on the recent finding of the Archaeopteryx fossil in Germany, scientists on the radio believe dinosaurs as a species evolved over millions of years into birds. Everything happens in increments, in tension with these imperceptible movements, which then suddenly become perceptible and gross.

White car, white car, white car.

Although it is currently thought that Archaeopteryx could sustain powered flight, it was probably not a strong flier; it may well have run, leaped, glided, and flapped all in the same day.

THE CUP on the floor is like my hand. My hand is just like my hand 5,000 years ago. The wind blows through the gills. A feeling of static, as if webbed lungs sliced the air moving through them. The cars going in and out of the tunnel of perception.

4 a.m. You swim through again and again to get to the laundry, sleeves full of wind, and then a wild cawing. Talons. Let the dreamer beware: the girl has no fins, no car, no love, her heart flapping. Is that a forest? Everything wants to talk. The air says *shhhh shhhh*. The light says *you can always turn back*. The worm says *my eye eyeless now*. The sharp smell of sweat mingles with dead skin and says *pa, pa, pa*. Your heart makes a *foom foom* sound—*Yes. Yes. Yes. Go. Go. Go.* The girl was stuck on her belly but her arms and legs grew long.

IN THE MORNING rain, birds, and the familiar loneliness. At lunch A sat next to me and asked for novel recommendations. *Tales of Burning Love* by Louise Erdrich, I said. Then I had to pretend I was a woman who had read *Tales of Burning Love* and not just a woman who had purchased the book with T five years ago. (Are masks what engender loneliness?)

I changed the topic to movies: 1. *Beloved* the movie couldn't capture how Sethe's history and horror live in the narrative present breath some couldn't finish the book (this astounded me). 2. The French movie I saw with S about the power of imagination and construction of story—oh we hate French movies so obsessive so circular no A loves them pass me a napkin. 3. The Italian comedy about the holocaust—G doesn't like the idea of the holocaust being humorized but I'm curious about our desire to find comedy in non-fictive horror and its link to survival and human evolution. 4. *Austin Powers* yuck but oh the scene where the tall blond girls fire missiles from their nipples.

PRIMAL. Yesterday, while walking home from the Castro, I had a premonition: *I am going to run into someone I know.* In the intersection of 16th Street and Market I saw V.

How are you? I asked.

Oh, I'm fine, she said, and then she told me about her sister's goat, and then she imitated the goat, laughing and fanning her long fingers at each side of her head. V is a full head taller than T was. She looks like a gangly, broad-shouldered teenager, or a muscular dark version of Patti Smith on the *Horses* album, her choppy black hair wagging in her angular face.

Two months ago she would have come back to my apartment and we'd have fucked in our jeans on the couch, these prehistoric sounds coming out of my throat—who knew those sounds were in me? V made me marvel at my own body; I thought anyone who could elicit such primal music would save me from something, the everyday, I guess. Once, we talked about adopting kittens and buying a house together, and then my imperceptible unhappiness evolved into gross unhappiness.

V lit a cigarette but did not give me her strong glare—only this faraway, disappointed look across the wilderness of Market Street as smoke drifted through the gap in her front teeth.

THERE IS NOTHING to be done about it. The bottom dark gray. And then it lightens by gradations and becomes the color of meringue. A white tennis shoe. Blizzard. Page. Piano keys. Above the building across from me now. A sphere of dusky condensation. Like a planet or a basketball. Dribbling edges and   — *Puff*—

Seventy to one hundred billion human beings have looked at clouds.

DR. R looks into Spot's eyes and purrs. She allows Dr. R to rest his chin on her head and probe for lumps and irregularities. He listens to her heart rhythms with his stethoscope and tells me she sounds good. Then he does the same with Fido, who plops into his hands as if she were filled with beans not muscle and blood. But when he takes the kittens' temperatures, Fido flips upside down mewling and Dr. R instructs me to immobilize her torso by placing my hands and forearms along her sides like a splint.

It reminds me of holding calves for my father while he branded their hind ends, the calf bucking its head and bellowing into my chest. Dr. R says good, that's good, in a soothing, melodic voice, and for just a moment I imagine Dr. R is my father and we are in a dark, hay-filled barn.

On my walk home up Dolores Street in the sun, while Spot presses her nose out the carry-box holes and Fido buries herself under the blanket, I think about the surprising softness of Dr. R's hands, how his knuckles are so beautifully couched in baby fat.

Man: You go that way. You go that way.

Woman: (dragging cardboard on sidewalk) I don't wanna go that way. Don't tell me to go that way.

Man: Which way do you want to go?

Woman: That way.

Man: Well, go that way, then.

Woman: No, don't tell me which way to go. I know where to go.

Man: Where are you going?

Woman: You don't have to know everything. You don't have to know where. Why do you need to know that, huh? Rick? Why do you always need to know everything? (crying)

Man: I'm going this way. You go wherever you want, okay? See, I'm walking away. (footsteps on 15th Street)

Woman: Don't go! Don't go!

PHENOMENON. On the fire escape a pigeon is pecking at the metal—there must be a bug on it. An orange line runs up the middle of the pigeon's black beak, as if someone had painted it on, and though the scientists would say it evolved for function not beauty, one has to wonder if the two can be separated. Take V's long hands for example. The pigeon walks sideways on the metal bar and sits there, soaking the sun into its feathers, a phenomenon that has been around for at least one hundred fifty million years. The pigeon is blinking. Blink. Blink. Last week a man on the radio said that while some birds have only a lower eyelid, pigeons use upper and lower lids to blink. They have monocular vision, which only allows them to see in two dimensions, and mostly what's in front of them, nothing in the periphery, nothing in depth. Every once in a while the pigeon fans or ruffles its feathers, evoking iridescent blues and greens.

NIGHT. Under the rose-flowered quilt my mother made for me I consider: 1. Fido's bloated belly and why she's so sluggish; 2. green, a dead tree, V's long back; 3. how pigeons developed an upper eyelid; 4. orange, yellow, and then this icy blue color I see reflecting off the windowpane.

Night vision. (*Tapetum lucidum.*) Spot stands on the rim of the tub and stretches up to reach a fly. She has the longest tail I've ever seen on a house cat. Dr. R says long tails are primordial; they enhance balance and hunting skills. Spot's tail approximates the tail of the first domestic cat, which would have descended from the African Wild Cat only twenty thousand years ago. Now she jumps from the floor almost to the top of the closet door. Sometimes she does this over and over—she looks like a skinny black something, I don't know what, her head pyramid shaped, gold eyes burning. A sphinx? An insect? What is the difference between an insect and a bug? Fido steps out onto the windowsill. That's new.

A cat has 230 bones in its body (humans have 206 bones). The extra bones may be the tail.

A cat will almost never meow at another cat; they use this sound for humans.

Cats and humans have an identical part of the brain for emotions.

The above fact is difficult to understand.

Cats can distinguish between red and green; red and blue; red and gray; green and blue; green and gray; blue and gray; yellow and blue, and yellow and gray. Yellow and red are indistinguishable.

A cat has a homing ability that uses its biological clock, the angle of the sun, and the Earth's magnetic field.

Cats have a third eyelid called a haw that is rarely visible. If it can be seen, it could indicate ill health.

Haw. Haw.

A cat's memory can last as long as sixteen hours—exceeding even that of monkeys and orangutans.

SEVEN THIRTY A.M. Saturday. A string has been cut between the world and me sometime during the night. This emotion, like the use of technology, seems distinctly human.

If I pick up the phone and dial someone my voice becomes the string. I force myself to lie in bed so that I can practice relaxing with paradox and ambiguity. I stare at the wall and blink like the pigeon. No haw.

I can't call anyone in the same time zone, anyway. Early morning calls are for crises, like when my mother or father dies. A 7:30 a.m. call would be dramatic.

What's wrong, are you all right? they'd say, and I'd have to confess that nothing is wrong.

It feels like a crime to be lonely.

The wall next to my bed is white and blank, except for a plastic oval placard of the Virgin Mary with her rose-colored heart outside her chest. She is pointing at it: to offer, to remind, to comfort, to bestow. Flames shoot out the top. The Virgin Mary is like Peter Falk in *Wings of Desire,* an imperceptible sustaining presence.

Norm Howard says we can expect highs of fifty-five and lows of forty degrees. Paul Schaeffer says a dog in Alabama dragged a sleeping man off a train track (call J). At 10 a.m. Click and Clack will talk about cars.

Tommy: Well, it's happened again.
Ray: What's happened, where? (laughter)

THE BUG has a soft black shell and red eyes, and it walks in the seam between the carpet and the wall, sometimes going up the wall in a drunken fashion. It disappears behind the radiator. Clifden Moth, earwig, true bug, ant yellow mother, cockroach, house cricket, glowworm, bush cricket, walking stick, squash bug, ground beetle, goat moth, leafhopper, rove beetle, tiger moth, ground bug, praying mantis, checkered beetle, honeybee, ladybug, weevil, human flea, horsefly, dragonfly, fire bug, diving beetle, stag beetle, hornet, caddis fly, longhorn beetle.

Two boys in Mormon suits and wearing backpacks walk toward Guerrero. They look clean, nice. They appear to have no grit or irony. One of them seems, for a moment, to offer a promise of sullenness, a slack in his walk, the hem of his pressed blue pants almost touching the sidewalk— but no, I think his shoe doesn't fit him.

APOLOGY. Oh. You blew food into my water, A said, and there it was, a piece of my rice floating in her water glass. Things like this used to make T laugh but they upset V—not that food would fly out of my mouth involuntarily, but that I wouldn't notice or seem to care. She felt it was disrespectful, and she may have been right. I quickly apologized to A.

Do you want a new glass? I asked. No, she said, smiling at me, that's perfectly all right. But then she inched her plate of chips and burrito closer to her chest. Her buoyant thirty-year-old arms seemed full of—what? Water? Possibilities?

EIGHT P.M. There is something new in my body. A new sound, a buzzing. Like a refrigerator motor. There it is. No, it's gone now.

8:30 p.m. Andrew dragged his futon from the giveaway space on the second floor where he dumped it last week back inside his apartment. Then he went back downstairs and left his door part way open. About half a foot. There are shadows, some light in the interior. The carpet in his studio is utilitarian gray, like mine. But this area has a yellowish tint, as if he spilled something, orange juice or lemon water. The papers that were stacked against the wall by his door are gone. The wall is the same off-white color as my walls. His room has a sound inside it, or at least it seems as if a sound leaks out, a low *wooooooo* or an *ooooooo*.

ANGLE. Cars cannot talk! Insistent. She doesn't know if this is the reason. Many marching men. Asphalt and green, but without a stroller. Can she run? The clip clip fades into air and then a discovery: That isn't what she said, this isn't who she is, this isn't her life—these aren't her shoes! Another day she will remember, but what? The color of your house, the angle of the sidewalk against that tree. One sound becomes another, long as a water hose. The delight of grasping—and over there a happy contingent of dogs, which is better than nothing on a cold day.

ON THE SIDEWALK, G reminded me of the Amish women in Newton Valley, Wisconsin, a certain prairie-like plainness and openness. Her hair pulled straight off her forehead and her broad face splotchy and red from crying. On the beach with her girlfriend she'd had a hard day. Another hard day.

She doesn't understand why I sit at home looking out my window. She doesn't understand why I am so passive about my sexuality.

G, I asked, do you ever wish you were a bird? I was thinking of the pigeon's ability to sit for hours and its precise yet limited vision, seeing only what is in front. I also was thinking of lifting off and floating above everything (and that I was attracted to A).

On the way home I stood on the M train. A woman in a trench coat and thick black glasses breathed on the side of my head when she talked. She had a red spot on her forehead. Behind me a man coughed and shifted so his hip fit above my hip; together we made one giant Muni-shaped puzzle. The woman had a low dry voice, she didn't believe in using hair driers, etc. Someone had had coffee recently. The man pushed air through his stomach, his breath surprisingly sour.

"The mind is wholly passive in the reception of all its simple ideas." (Locke)

GONE. On the gray carpet outside the bathroom door I studied my bare feet in the air, while over the phone A told me about her childhood on a cotton farm outside Stoneville, Virginia, and her hippie parents who had money but lived without running water and electricity. They were crazy, she said. A doesn't get ruffled, her face is wide and still: she is like beach sand, or cotton. Even when her dog runs away down 24th Street, an event I witnessed a month ago when G and I visited her at her apartment, she stays calm. She was eating (maybe a sandwich?), and on the phone her steady, devout crunching began to sound as if an animal were chewing the phone line.

A, I said, do you know that I'm physically attracted to you?

No, I didn't know that, she said, and she stopped chewing.

Do you have any of those feelings for me? I asked.

Pause. Still no chewing.

Did you know, she asked, that to grow the fiber for one cotton diaper requires over 105 gallons of water?

I didn't know that. She continued. One T-shirt needs over 250 gallons, a bath towel over 400, a man's dress shirt 415, and almost a million gallons of water for a pair of jeans.

That's a lot of water, I said.

Yes it is, she said and she breathed into the phone. I could hear her put her fork down, a barely perceptible clink.

A tangerine-colored Corvette blares wild rock while all the beige cars go quietly to their intersection.

NIGHT CARS sound different than day cars. The dark air muffles the sound. And then everything changes. I put on my pajamas and recognize myself in the mirror. Fifty-two days left of being thirty-eight. On my way to the bathroom a quick, reckless thought about people who drive noisy vehicles, though sometimes I wish I could roar over the Dolores Street hills, waking all the monks, defying the pavement in that moment of acceleration and suspension when the metal lifts.

Woman: Take this for me. (crinkling sound)

Man: What do you need this for? You don't need this, do you?

Woman: Oh, please don't say that, Rick. Please just.

Man: All I mean is, no listen. It's not going to.

Woman: You don't know that, nobody knows.

Man: Where are you going now?

Woman: Over there with this, if you won't. You never will.

Man: I didn't say never, I didn't say it. I mean I would but I don't understand why, alls I asked was *why*.

Woman: Why why why why why why why whywhywhywhywhy whywhywhywhywhy…

Man: (shouting over her) Let's start over, okay?

ANDREW is talking to someone in the hall, but his words go down, they fall on the carpet. Andrew stands at the top of the stairs and the other man, who sprouts black curls under a yellow bicycle helmet, stands on the step below him and looks up at him, as if he's looking *for* him. Andrew doesn't look at him; he looks at the wall next to his door. The man is trying to locate him, but Andrew is a master of dislocation, an irregular pattern—he's there but not there; his voice emanates from the carpet. Look at him, Andrew!

The man leans forward to say something and places his hand on Andrew's forearm. He takes his hand away. He straps on his helmet and walks down the stairs. Andrew mumbles goodbye and remains in the hall at the top of the stairs like an after shadow, staring into the space where the man was, perhaps seeing the disruption of air molecules or whatever it is we leave behind.

BEAUTIFUL. Someone on the radio quotes Mina Loy, who said consciousness has no climax, and I think about what that means. We have ten billion brain neurons, sixty trillion connections. Unique states of consciousness: 5.9 billion. I picture consciousness as a mass of gray thoughts, like gray dots. An ocean. A field. Everything has equal weight— which may be freedom. No rising tensions and crisis action scenes. No adrenalin rushes. No epiphanies or hope for resolution. Just dot after dot after dot. Or is it a redefinition or a re-weighting of action?

Another white car gliding through the intersection.

It would be sad, D says, if we lost all big drama. But we are uncertain if trauma necessarily leads to drama. Trauma is inevitable, but drama is when we blow it up with meaning and emotion through language. Drama is a balloon.

UNDERNEATH. The drunken man was leaning against a building and watching S as we walked toward him. She was wearing her peach fur coat and gold bell-bottoms. It was dark, but in the streetlight her eyelids shone with glitter. She didn't see the man watching her, she was laughing and telling me a story about the mice that had invaded her apartment. She set live traps and caught two mice, but then she couldn't drown them, which is the nicest way to kill them, and now at night she hears the mice in her kitchen eating peanuts and playing mahjong. S was holding her mouth the way she does when she's telling a story, as if the vowels and consonants must be shaped against the mouth's roof, as if her well-shaped teeth must mold each syllable and then roll them out. She was still talking as we walked in front of the man. He hid his face behind his hands—it was a sudden motion—and even though I didn't think she was paying attention, S jumped back, and her mouth went slack, and a completely new look took over her face. Something underneath came forward: S's face opened up and exposed a blankness. An ocean, a field. Perception gone feral.

DREAM. You are at a party and friends touch your head: oh, it goes like that? A long carpeted room and a room within that room you didn't know was there looking out on a lawn so green it becomes light. No one says you have to get up.

Climb stairs. People inside a room—you can go in or turn your head. These Mafia types. Everyone laughing and stretching their mouths. (So far no antidepressants but tall wet grass.) Thump thump. A band of cats hurtle themselves against the doors. One cat blows a hole through an owl. God doesn't care what you wear. Man and woman hold hands swinging desperately, it's a day for couples, everyone you know is in love.

GONE. The divisions seem arbitrary. Or are they essential?
Them there. Me here.
They're just over there. I'm just over here. There. Here. Here. There.
V just drove by again. V's black Honda. (Never T's blue Horizon.)
For a moment, I wish I could have stayed. I press my forehead against the window.

Night. My neighbor upstairs is walking around in his living room. He only exists in sound, I have no other evidence, have never seen him. He stomps insensibly from his kitchen to his bedroom and then from his bedroom to his kitchen and back again. Unlaced hiking boots. I imagine a wash of greasy brown hair and pasty skin, broad shoulders and hips, pudgy knees. It really doesn't make any sense. Finally he turns on the television. A monk in a brown robe crosses 15th Street.

SOUND. From the kitchen she hears something behind her. Footsteps. She came home late and is not sure she locked the door. A sound behind her, in the hallway, someone breathing. Someone is in the apartment, she realizes, and slowly closes the refrigerator door.

"Who is it?" she asks.

The intruder walks through her living room toward her bedroom. She can hear her file drawers slide open. She wonders if she will have time to climb out the kitchen window onto the fire escape. She wonders if the kitchen window will open, or if the frame will stick because she has never opened it. Why has she never opened the kitchen window? Why can't she focus on the important tensions in this scene?

More sounds. The intruder is going through her dresser, the bottom drawer full of journals. Silence. Is the intruder reading her journals? She wants to know if he's admiring them. She reminds herself that the intruder has the power to harm her—he might kill her if he has a gun. Her heart pounds appropriately. He probably has a gun, why not?

She hears more footsteps, heavy landings, and she imagines hiking boots, a tall heavy man. She looks out the kitchen window again; a pigeon sits on the fire escape like an omen. Her only hope is to climb down the fire escape. She pushes up on the window. The window does not budge; it is painted shut. She is trapped. She hears the intruder hauling something across her living room, the sound of fabric against fabric.

Her bed!

The intruder is taking her bed!

Why would he take her bed?

Well, what does she value more than her bed?

She runs out and sees the end of her mattress sliding into the hallway. "Stop," she yells. He flips the end of the mattress and the corner slams her in the face, sending her reeling into the coffee table. Pain shoots through the side of her head. Blackness. Except for dots of red and orange and blue.

When she wakes up her cats are licking the blood off her face. The End.

Wait.

Doesn't she want to catch the mattress thief?

Who would risk her life for a mattress?

Perhaps the intruder kills one of her cats. This would raise the stakes—the stakes must be raised!—as her students say in every workshop. She begins smoking and drinking and then picks up a venereal disease but is too ashamed to go to the doctor. She dies slowly and crazily, like King Henry the Eighth, of syphilis, though it may have been lead poisoning. Or maybe she does go after the intruder and he shoots her in the belly and she bleeds to death on Market Street. The End.

6 p.m. A luminescent white bug is crawling across the page, along the blue line. It crawls only along the blue line, as if the blue is a road leading somewhere definite. The bug crawls to the end of the page, then turns back and follows the blue line back to the other side.

Man: This isn't a ditch I'm willing to die in, but if I had to bet if the tomb were empty or not, I'd bet not.

Woman: (throwing a stone into the street) They wouldn't have mentioned an empty tomb unless there was an empty tomb, Rick.

Man: It had nothing to do with his corpse or an empty tomb.

Woman: You don't know that, you always talk as if you know that.

Man: He didn't die for me, that's what. He died for his passion for social justice. He had a vocation to do the right thing.

Woman: What would it hurt to sing it anyway; you never will sing with me.

TEN P.M. Andrew is going out again—maybe to meet the man who was here in the bicycle helmet. His door opens, closes. Footsteps down the stairs. He does not cross 15th Street.

D is turning fifty this year and she says she has lost her sense of sensuality. I suggest she look under the bed. But then she says she always needs something in her mouth, which sounds sensual to me. We talk about whether movies, television, radio, music, shopping, concerts, romantic relationships, sex, pinball, roller skating, video games, computer games, reading, writing, language aren't a distraction from emptiness. We don't know. We talk about certainty.

Then she asks me if I'm tracking this moment for my dailiness project.

Later, when I am supposed to be writing, I go out into the hall with the mouse-bird. The African Wild Cat hunts at night, but is known for some crepuscular activity. Andrew has not come home yet. There is no sound near his door. Spot tears into the mouse as usual, but Fido lounges like an evolutionary mutant on her side, just inside my door.

11 p.m. Another late cold front blowing in from Alaska. Inland highs of forty-five, lows might reach thirty, so, cover your winter shrubs and succulents.

Heat also escapes through walls, floors, and ceilings, at a rate proportioned to the conducting power of the substances of which they are composed. In many cultures, rugs are placed on the floor to prevent unnecessary losses of heat as well as give the home a warm, cozy feeling.

SIX FEET is the length of my couch. The space from the couch to my red writing table by the window is seven and a half feet.

At Cost Plus I told S I'm not sure I have the skills to buy the right rug. S said, That's ridiculous. How can a person who's going to be forty years old not have the skills to buy a rug? I said it was a good question, but that I was only going to be thirty-nine. S couldn't be burdened with this detail and walked off down the garden aisle to buy some plant holders.

One rug sported purples and greens, the other rose, blue, and orange. I paced around the first rug, then the second. I put my nose to the fabric because certainly one can't make a major household decision with only one sense. I walked fifteen feet away and climbed on the garden bucket shelf for an aerial view. A matted-haired saleswoman kept her eye on me. S walked up and put her hand on my leg: You can do it, she said, by way of apology for her earlier abruptness, I believe. Finally, I shut my eyes and chose the rosy one and S exclaimed, the way only S can exclaim, completely genuine and indulgent, Oh, that's a gorgeous absolutely perfect rug for you!

ALL THE B's are blue. *Baby, baby, baby.* The A's are pink. The letters with a tail are red. The word *pillow* floats over your wrist and out the window, gold. The sound of wind gallops a blue horse. The street song a far-off keening—but not like that, like this! Farther off another story: someone raking silver into piles. Wouldn't you like to be called wee one again? Think about it. Staring out into the gray light—and now inky shadows walk into the room. *Baby, baby, baby.* In the middle of the night you speak in colors, your tongues green.

"Where light meets darkness, colors flash into existence. Colors are, therefore, the offspring of the greatest polarity our universe can offer." (Zajonc)

PAIN SETTLING into my shoulder now? Inside the body, outside the body. These thoughts at 3 p.m. in an ordinary afternoon full of moments. I meditate for twenty minutes and then smell something burning in a place I can't locate.

FIDO PLOPS herself on my foot along with questions of privacy: Who owns event and memory and who owns that which flows in and out of our consciousness. If consciousness can be singular. (Tom Waits upstairs again.) I am not Henry Miller or Anais Nin—or am I? "We know two kinds of things about what we call our psyche (or mental life): firstly, its bodily organ and scene of action, the brain (or nervous system) and, on the other hand, our acts of consciousness, which are immediate data and cannot be further explained by any sort of description." Said Freud. —A delicate brunette woman peeks around the corner as if she's being stalked.

From a geo-historical view human life may be the blink of a pigeon's eye.

And yet the minutes feel awfully personal while sitting in a chair in front of a draft in front of a window.

A cat's memory can last as long as sixteen hours—exceeding even that of monkeys and orangutans.

NIGHT. J is sitting next to me on my new rug. He bends down and puts his face close to mine, inches away, so I am looking directly into his light brown eyes, and for a moment—a flash instant—I can see in his milky irises and black pupils his seriousness and despair and wildness. How to explain this—I see fear and the opposite of fear, death and the opposite of death. Equally weighted. My chest tightens.

Night. Two whites and a red almost collide; more colors now, people starting to try to get home.

What is V doing tonight? J says sex is dead. He won't explain it.

The new rug is soft; Spot and Fido drape themselves over my legs. Spot offers me her black pyramid-shaped face and we kiss.

IDENTITY. A mother and two young boys cross Dolores Street pushing an empty stroller. If I say woman instead of mother, what does that do—detach her from responsibility? Or free her identity? And once our identities are freed, then what? Perhaps we roam like ghosts, like the Native American man in the 1600s who was brought into a city and for the rest of his life believed he was dead. Or perhaps we go underground and stay pure like the ground squirrel.

The radio says Chevron is responsible for poisoning thousands of people in a village in Nigeria. I should call the police; instead, I arrange the oranges in my new ceramic tray (a gift from J) on the counter, toss the rotten expensive organic broccoli in the vegetable bin. Though I don't think it will help, I write in a voice I don't recognize another letter to my congresswoman. *As a constituent of your district, I urge you to take action...*

WATER. S has styled and dyed her hair a burgundy color that matches her lipstick and lifts the green light from her face; in the dark of the car she looked like an Andy Warhol painting. No, Van Gogh.

(That's what we see from the front part of our faces but at the back a blur and a jumble.)

She kept looking at her hair in the rearview mirror as she drove, and then when she stopped at a red light, out of her glove compartment she pulled a Wet Wipe and ran it through her hair, flattening and shaping it around her right ear.

I said, I have never seen or imagined anyone styling hair with a Wet Wipe. She laughed, but her black eyes glistened, suddenly teary. Sometimes S's interior rides so close to her exterior; it's like she's a bowl of water with shiny objects floating on top and a whole other murky world an inch below.

On the dance floor, we met G and other people, and S whirled for us—her red velvet skirt floated around her pink panties, the black light flaring, the red skirt breathing, and S became one of those neon-lit jellyfish that V and I saw at the Monterey Aquarium, wafting open, clamping shut. The oldest living creature in the sea.

The sky shifts from blue to black to blacker. A woman with a yellow plastic rose in her hat leans against one of the garages across from my building. She lifts her arm and says hello to invisible people. Perhaps Peter Falk is touching her sleeve.

Jellyfish do not have brains, hearts, bones, or eyes.

Not so much a mystery, as a nerve net, which consists of receptors capable of detecting light, odor, and other stimuli and coordinating appropriate responses.

Some jellyfish, like the sea wasp, descend to deeper waters during the bright sun of the midday. They surface early morning, late afternoon, and evening.

It is 10 a.m. and I am hungry.

Zooplankton, crustaceans, occasionally other jellyfish.

Jellyfish drift upon ocean currents, tides, and wind for horizontal movement.

What do they think of aquarium walls?

Spadefish, sunfish, loggerhead turtles, and other marine organisms eat them.

Jellyfish have been around for more than 650 million years, outdating dinosaurs and sharks.

Jellyfish are over 95 percent water.

You are 80 percent water.

I was stung in the face by a jellyfish. True or False.

DREAM. It really doesn't matter. We love, we sleep, we dream. We live in a big house with a long kitchen and a stainless steel oven. People from the past show up—you've invited them—a mother and many children. It's raining. They bring orange juice and there's white wine left over. The videographer can't come. You think you have nothing to offer, forgot to go to the store. You have invited them to an event for which you haven't prepared. Shame becomes a torso.

Two girls under six running in the rain. It's flooding. She'll be swept down the street—look—her ball is rolling across the black street through inches of water. The girls run into invisibility.

THE KITTEN SITTER is tall and round shouldered, and she's wearing clunky black shoes that make her tower over me in a cute, dorky way. She reminds me of my niece, who reminds me of myself when I was twenty. The shoes are supposed to make the kitten sitter look cool, along with the seventies or is it eighties country western shirt and plaid pants, but she is not cool and I am glad. Her hair is growing out—it seems like all the young girls in San Francisco have decided in unison to grow out their hair so they can clamp it off their faces with big plastic clips. The kitten sitter uses bobby pins. It all doesn't come together beautifully. She moves awkwardly like a newborn goat whose body is always a surprise. For a moment, while we stand in the narrow hall that is my kitchen and she stares at the letters and photos and Post-its covering my wall, I imagine pressing my hand against her sternum in a gesture of dominance and possession, which would frighten us both. Instead I show her the trick of easing open the refrigerator so she won't pop the freezer door off onto her foot, and I show her the cupboard of kitten food and tortilla chips and canned tuna and garbanzo beans, and I show her the blender, in case she's into blending. She nods and hulks over me and I feel ancient.

I should offer her tea. Do you want some tea?

And when she sits on my couch her knees reach the red-painted edge of the coffee table.

We drink Good Earth tea and she says she eats macaroni and cheese, and I think I will buy macaroni and cheese for her. She will be in my mind like a daughter or niece, and I will fill the cupboards with macaroni and cheese. When I'm gone she will lie on my little couch and watch movies all day and snoop through my drawers and files and drape herself in my plastic jewelry.

At least I hope she does. I hope she goes through every drawer and all my books and reads my journals. (Though in a moment this impulse, like the predatory one before it, will pass.)

PHOSPHORESCENCE. A topographical view standing in green surrounded by other people standing in green and the weather, the air. Rain. Snow. Breeze. We get wet and shiny. The birds sound like ducks. The birds are ducks.

The woman on the radio says the spirit wants to float and sit and breathe, but the soul wants to salsa and tell stories. The sound of this statement pleases me, but I don't believe it. Perhaps the difference is theological. Or perhaps the woman can feel in a way that I cannot the difference between spirit and soul.

A dark, shadowy ceiling, a grayness that seems soluble. Drink a glass of soymilk, climb back into bed—a flock of birds breaks open off the electrical wire.

THE BIRDS in the palm trees on Dolores Street screech for what sounds to my human senses like joy, but it could also be a warning…

SOMEONE IS KNOCKING at Andrew's door. A fat bald man, made foggy by the peephole glass. He turns and looks at my door; his face is round and pink and pleasant, and above his forehead waft strands of light gray wiry hair. He looks at my door for a long time; he seems to be looking directly at me, which causes my breath to speed up and my shoulders to tighten. He turns and knocks again. And then he takes paper and pen out of his pocket and writes something. He slides it under Andrew's door. I imagine it says: *your neighbor across the hall is a voyeur.*

MOONLIGHT. 10 p.m. Cars shadow the ceiling. A brown car stops at 15th Street, a burly man's arm hanging out the window with a cigarette. He just sits there. Another brown car goes around him. Why is he sitting there? Why doesn't he cross Dolores and go on with the rest of his life?

11 p.m. Where are the sponges? (In the yellow bucket.) The sill turns creamy white and begins to shine. And there: dirt in the corners. I scour them with a toothbrush. I hang out the window into the night and hurl buckets of hot water with vinegar against the glass; the water catches in milky light and then rains down on the sidewalk.

MYTHOLOGICAL. A giant raccoon lumbers out from an alley and stands upright with its front legs spread wide in a challenging gesture, as if it were half raccoon half human. The raccoon seems to be about three feet tall. From inside its black mask gold eyes glare at me; it reminds me of V glaring, and it also reminds me of that Clint Eastwood movie, *Unforgiven*, in which they all bite it by gunfire. The raccoon and I stand there as if in a high noon showdown, except the evening air is dim and the sidewalk is wide enough for a herd of us. An inexplicable primal animosity builds inside me; I cross my arms and stare back.

The raccoon's face is wide and round as a Frisbee. A coat of street light, like dust, covers its fur, the light catches its fingernails and top row of yellow teeth, and the wind ruffles the raccoon's fur, which makes the raccoon stand up taller and puff itself up, yes like a raccoon centaur—or no—like Mae West with her full bosom and cinched waist, or Marlon Brando or—like Ralph in *The Honeymooners* puffing himself up.

ANTS HAVE APPEARED in the kitchen. In from the rain through the cupboard crack near the window, a line of brown ants crawl across the back of the counter, behind my *Eat Thee Wild Things* and *Moosewood* cookbooks, which I never use, and the dish drainer. Spot crouches on the cupboard and stares at them, her eyes tracing the line back and forth. At the drainer there is a diaspora, groups of ants breaking off and climbing up the faucet, onto the faucet handles, into the sink. Ants running up and down the sink, back and forth along the metal edge in unison. They are a unit. It's as if there is a string connecting them.

THE DAY a refraction of sunlight. Ducks, geese, sky. V and I sat on a bench and threw chunks of bread near the shore. There were two small black ducks and some big ducks. V aimed her crumbs at the little ones, but the big ones shamelessly gobbled them up.

One chocolate brown duck had a squarish head. I pointed and said, Look at that one brown duck with a squarish head.

Why, V said in a challenging tone. What's wrong with a square head?

No, I tried to explain, the head is fine because of its squareness; its squareness is unexpected, unusual, and therefore a disruption.

Its head is a disruption! she yelled. And she was glaring like the giant raccoon, and of course it wasn't at all like in my fantasies. V sees me as the big duck that swims forward and gobbles up the bread. V is the little duck, I am the big shallow duck. So, of course, she had to criticize me, find ways to shrink me to manageable size. She'd tell you a different story.

Look, I tried again, you can see my breath, and your breath, and the duck's breath. We couldn't see the duck's breath in reality, but we knew it was breathing.

V began haa-haaing her breath into the air and white puffs came out. The sun was flaring up across the lake. From around the paved bend, a girl with long black braids rolled up on her plastic three-wheeler and stopped about five feet behind our bench.

What is she staring at? V asked.

Nothing, I said. She wants to know what kind of human beings we are.

What kind are we? V asked.

I don't know, I said. I guess we're the kind that sit on benches and throw bread at ducks. She opened her mouth very wide and laughed.

NOTES. The Safeway cart clangs on the street again, the man hollering a lament—Jo-seph! Jo-seph! Jo-seph! Jo-seph!—until the syllables become merely high and low notes, a mid and low C passing by my window.

SUNLIGHT. Dr. R is explaining that Fido was born without grooves in her back leg bones to hold her knee joints in place; her knee joints float over the leg muscles, which is why she does not display normal hunting behaviors (stalking, jumping, chasing). In the wild she would have been eaten or starved. A surgeon could carve grooves out for her, he says, but she probably will still suffer from early joint deterioration and arthritis.

While describing the leg's architecture and the surgery, he takes my hand and guides it over Fido's back legs, and I nod, but I am distracted by the warm fat of Dr. R's hands; the warmth is like one of those penetrating rays in science fiction movies, and suddenly I am blind and Dr. R is my Braille teacher. I am sitting in the sunlight in a classroom for the blind and he is standing behind me leading my hand over white bumps and breathing his kindness into the side of my head. I open my eyes; Fido on her belly is pawing my wrist. Poor Fido. Dr. R hands me a tissue from his metal stand and I say I will think about the surgery, but we know I won't think about it much because its prognosis is poor. On the walk home, the sidewalks are shining because the sidewalk makers mixed ground quartz into the concrete.

WAWANA NA ELVES NA AH, he says, when I ask Mr. Petpourri about dietary supplements for cat joint deterioration. He seems to have shrunk. His grayish brown beard falls below the counter—he may be sitting on a low chair, or he may be standing. Usually he sits on a high chair, and I can see his whole head, beard, and shoulders. He seems to be shrugging, his neck disappears and his upper beard wags.

Could you repeat that? I ask, and Mr. Petpourri says again, Wawana na elves na ah.

We look at each other, or rather, I look at him to detect any other clues as to the meaning, but he has already departed by gazing out the storefront window. His eyes are green, the color of a pale green Frigidaire, and they are un-lifed, like eyes set in the head of a stuffed deer, or like the eyes of a plastic elf that has weathered in the garden. I think I am going to ask him again about the supplements, about his bearded language, but instead of words coming out of my mouth I hear a small squeak, like the squeak of a toy. Mr. Petpourri's beard jumps—he is pulled from his misery just long enough to see me. But there is nothing for us to do. Language has failed us. We go silently on with our day.

TOPOGRAPHICAL anxiety. A two-legged horse eating grass, and you in the center of the ring without your whip. The event is sold out, but no one has paid for the tickets. You look under their coats—for what? Stage directions. Two girls summersault through the outdoor wedding, hair and dresses flapping. Applause, applause!

Long table and microphones—and then the announcement that your legs are not too long? Which way, you ask, and now you are riding the horse in your white veil, you want it to gallop but it can only fly.

TEN P.M. The fat bald man is knocking on Andrew's door again; he knocks on Andrew's door, and then he looks over at my door. Andrew must be gone for the holidays? No opening and closing sounds from his apartment. He hasn't been in the halls, or walking on Market Street. There is no smell outside his apartment. But there is a sound—not the *woooo* sound, something else. The door is cold against my ear. A clicking, like someone turning something on, or winding something up. It could be his radiator. Now silence. A creaking? The note the man left on his first visit, just the edge of it, is visible under the door. The white ruffled edge of spiral notebook paper.

TEN P.M. The bald man is at Andrew's door again, and again he looks at my door. Why does the bald man look at my door? Why do I stand at the peephole and look at the bald man? I am coaxing my brain to give me the expression on the bald man's face when he looked at my door the first time, seven days ago, and then the second time, and then this time, now. He looks contemplative, thoughtful—as if he's measuring something.

The bald man is short and pear-shaped. His earlobes are extraordinarily long and make his ears look like musical instruments. He knocks on Andrew's door again, this time more loudly, and he presses his ear to the door. He looks older than Andrew, much older the more I look at him. Is he Andrew's father? Is he Andrew's brother? Lover? Uncle? Cousin? Teacher? Friend? Social worker? He hangs outside the door for a few moments, and then he trots down the stairs.

IN JAPAN teenage boys are shutting themselves inside their bedrooms; they live in their bedrooms for years playing games on their computers and inventing computer programs. One boy kidnapped a nine-year-old girl and kept her in his room for a year, just for company. What about the parents? I ask. The parents must know the boys are in there. They must be feeding them. Oh, they know, she says, but what can they do? We argue about what they could do, D saying that no one can force a teenage boy to do anything and me saying that the whole family is complicit and should go to jail though D reminds me that staying in one's room is not a crime.

GONE. The halls are empty. My fingernails are not long enough to grasp the note by the frayed edges. I get a table knife and slip it under the door and try to coax the note out, but it slides back half an inch. I need something like a tweezers, but I can't find one so I fashion a tweezers-like appliance from a pair of black chopsticks I never use that V gave me—red dragons painted on the black. I pinch the note and slide it under the door.

Andy, give me a call when you get this note. Richard

The script is dark and tiny, written in black ink, by someone who presses hard on his d's and g's. The paper smells like pocket lint. I slip it back under the door.

10 p.m. I think I hear a glass being put down in a sink. A cough. Nothing. More nothing that sounds a lot like a glass being put down in a sink and a cough.

I could be filling in nothing with something. Maybe this something is delusion. Meanwhile Andrew is decomposing and alone in there. I imagine his small hands tucked under his chin.

THREE A.M. His studio cocoon is lit by moonlight; the entire apartment is about the size of my living room. A door to the right hangs open to a large utility closet; another shut door must lead to the bathroom. Along the wall to the left a mini stove, refrigerator, and sink. Three glasses sit in the sink. Blocks of newspapers are stacked around the bed—he must climb over them to get to the bathroom. Behind the bed bookshelves cover the wall from floor to ceiling, a few shelves devoted to model ships and boats. The bed is covered with a dark blue duvet, and it is empty.

I climb down from the fire escape, drop to the sidewalk, and return the leaning ladder to the laundry room.

D says call the police. But that seems drastic. What would I say? I call G and S and H and they all say essentially what my mother said to me once a week for fifteen years: you are making a mountain of a molehill. He's probably gone for the holidays. (D notes that this entire project and half the art of narrative depend on making mountains out of molehills.)

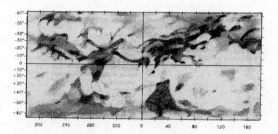

ON MUNI I bend over to release the pressure on my spine and in the lens of my glasses see colors like a stained glass window, an arch of white over blocked colored lights. In the right lens a mirage of red bursting out of green and brown, kaleidoscoping into a red flower, green windmill. I lift my head and the blood rushes down into my stomach. Someone glances at me, a swimmer coming up for air.

YOU LIE IN THE SUN just like a girl lying in the sun. That horn honks just like a horn. Someone is running toward you. That motorcycle is just like that woman's voice. That pair of slippers is just like that word you can't remember and even if you could you wouldn't be able to pronounce it. That pile of work waiting to be done is just like that wooden bench on which the dog's nose rests. The sun is going to run out. That wind is blowing like wind blows everywhere. You wore slippers shaped like rats; they make you the Big Cheese. The dog sits closer now. The wind leans in, its snout resting on one paw. The sun leans in and opens one eye, the color of champagne.

THE SOUND is back. Not like a refrigerator motor but like the sound of a plane far off or the sound of cells dividing.

Yesterday, X appeared outside Harvest Market in a blue hat on which she'd sewn cloth flowers. She introduced me to a handsome woman with brown eyes. The woman leaned down and asked my name in a deep-sea voice that shot directly into my muscles.

Oh, that's a nice name, she said.

X went home, but the woman and I ate lunch on the sidewalk benches. She chewed slowly. She came back to my house and we sat on the couch and talked. She has a mass of black hair that sits slightly askew, or perhaps she was tilting her head, or perhaps her head was askew. I said, I have never seen anything like your hair, and she leaned back with one arm on the top of the couch and her hair mass leaned with her.

Do you want a glass of water? I asked

Her hand wrapped all the way around the blue glass.

We walked through Dolores Park to the train and the sky was hot blue and the grass was green and the woman talked about motion and light.

While crossing the park for the second time, she said she had been thinking of moving back to San Francisco (she lives in New York and was flying home that evening).

Yes, do that, I said.

For a moment as we stood on the glimmering concrete I imagined leaning forward and pressing my lips to the back of her hand, but instead I leaned forward and pressed my lips to her lips. She opened her mouth. The train was careening down Church Street hill.

THE SOUND has grown louder, how can I describe it?—adrenaline and endorphins sluicing up and down my spine and central nervous system. How many millions of years has this been happening to us?

And there are the clouds—big, puffy, impervious condensations roving over my head, the roof, the city.

Spot flies over the coffee table her primordial tail knocking a glass of water and my books to the floor.

Big orange school bus rounds the corner off Dolores down 15th Street—that doesn't usually happen.

"—the everyday still has some surprises in store for us." (LeFebvre)

Man: Did you hear that? Listen to that. (silence)

Woman: Telling him that, telling him that.

Man: You know it. You know what.

Woman: Look at this, Rick. I found it yesterday, in the somewhere, you know.

Man: Oh, man, don't make me look at that again.

Woman: It has these soft places, like this, see? You can see through them. Can you see me, Rick? (laughter)

Man: (laughter)

WHAT DO YOU THINK about recycling souls, the body disposable, consciousness infinite? A brown ant is crawling up my forearm, trekking through dark blond hairs. It climbs up a hair, the weight bending the hair into a U. The ant climbs off and around another hair, steadily making its way toward my shirtsleeve. Later, the ant is running along the neckline of my sweater, running back and forth as if looking for an entrance, and then suddenly along my shoulder, its two-bulbed body racing up and down the side seam like trickling black blood.

The woman called. I could hear her breathing into the phone between words. She said she hopes to see me again when she returns to the city next month. She worries about her fish. She has a fish tank and she bought snails to keep the tank clean. She said she thinks humans have an incredible capacity to kill tropical fish. One snail in particular seems to be working hard, sidling up the glass, leaving no trace of slime or fish food debris. The guppies flit between green filaments, a flash of blue-green and then another flash.

Later I lie in bed and imagine I plant my face on the tank glass and the fish swim for my eyeballs. I whisper *you you you* and they tread outside the cave of my mouth.

GOOD. The reverend from Tibet is wearing thick black glasses that cover half his face. When he looks up at me I feel like I'm seeing him through a car windshield, like he's a child in the backseat staring out at the world and I'm on the sidewalk waving.

We walk past the tulips, up the stairs. The reverend's head swivels to look at the officer on a motorbike. A cigarette wrapper blows over his path; he takes it in. He glances at his watch. As we walk slowly past the swing sets and plastic tubes, the children in the sandbox stare up at him, their shovels in the air.

The air around him softens, like it does around fountains and children. In the middle of the block, between Sanchez and Noe, he stops suddenly and leans toward me. His eyes are as black as the rim of his glasses.

Do you sleep? He asks.

He smiles at me the way a tree or swing or bench would smile, and for a moment I imagine taking the reverend's lovely Tibetan head off his neck and tucking it under my arm, or maybe carrying his head in one of those scarf slings, the way Laotians carry babies.

Yes, I assure him. I sleep.

Okay, he says. Good.

I WAKE UP thinking about the woman and the kiss, and then D calls and says that I should turn on the radio because scientists are saying they lost the water on mars. (They had found water, but now they can't find it.) D is happy that I met someone but unhappy that the woman lives in New York. The distance seems un-navigable, doesn't it? she asks, and I say nothing because I am thinking about the fact of the woman's tongue and that this transcends geography. I tell D that the tongue transcends geography, and she laughs, and the phone flies out of her hand. Later she reminds me that V's long back transcended her short temper for a whole year and that's true.

SPOT. Now that she is dead, I can see the name did not suit her at all. It didn't do justice to her primordial long tail, or her relentless extraordinary jumping, or her regal tiptoeing across my face, or her prowess with the mouse and string games. Her name should have been something fierce and with more dignity, like Xuela or Delphine.

My teeth hurt. A wind on the back of my neck and this hurtled feeling. Arms and legs and torso back in an earlier place.

At first I thought it was Fido, because it just seemed right that if one of them were going to die suddenly, it would be grooveless Fido.

She's on the roof now, wrapped in a bed blanket, lying in a wicker basket.

Dr. R said it was a blood clot in her brain or a heart attack.
But she's only a kitten, I said.

NIGHT and I can see my fingerprints on the clean window, a pattern of smudges around the bottom panes where I pull the window up, and under the top sill where I sometimes push the window even higher so it's wide open. The streets are empty, except for darkness and parked cars.

"They give birth astride of a grave, the light gleams an instant, then it's night once more." (Beckett)

AT THE EDGE of the parking lot at Green Gulch Zen Center, a fawn stands under a birch tree, branch shadows playing across its back and limbs. The fawn is the color of caramels. No—it is the color of the drought grass. The fawn stares at me, a lifting, a golding, the fawn an alchemist. Back legs tent; front legs turn out like Andrew's do. Tufts of grayish, whitish fur fan out from its belly and forelegs.

Water somewhere. Trickling.

A doe trots in the wooded area next to the parking lot, spindly legged and exuberant. Crackling leaves. The deer looks up at me with the eyes of a monk. Stop. She prickles her way along the edge of the asphalt, lifting her hooves as if each time is new, as if born again at the beginning of each step because her brain isn't burdened by the catalog of experience.

Now. Now. Now. The doe lifts a leg, holding her hoof in the air like a bell.

I AM THINKING about the impossibility of capture or representation or evocation of experience with language, how language doesn't owe anything to experience, how language has its own story. I am thinking about what the monk, who is also a doctor of philosophy, said today about the phenomenology of experience, the constant refusal and concealment of the world amidst the open region, quoting Heidegger or M. Merleau Ponty, neither of whom were Buddhists. I am too tired to look it up and I am not supposed to be reading or writing on this retreat. There is the event in its time, and then there is the languaging of this event to create a cohesive object. A body. Words. Event and body. Not the same thing at all.

For example, I have not given you a single sunrise or sunset. My windows face north. I have seen numerous sunsets on the streets, or on hills, or at the beach. All the beach moments I've omitted, or they've omitted themselves. I don't know why. Form, or perhaps language, demanded it. A whole trip to Massachusetts where I dug someone's garden and petted her sows—the heat and vibration made us stand still for a long time, made me think of the color tan, made us laugh and sing a song about pigs—barred. Omission makes a day.

THE PIGEON on my fire escape drops to the windowsill and walks into my apartment. She stands on the sill bobbing her head, eyes darting from my computer to my bed and then she steps onto the cat tree and pecks at the carpet. Meanwhile the birds outside are going crazy. Pigeons cooing. Then the sound of an owl. The parrots in the palm trees on Dolores screech—and it sounds completely different in this weather!

Ten minutes later, right before Fido lopes in from the hall and sprawls across my leg, the pigeon steps back to the sill and hops down. Now, walking back and forth on the telephone high wire that crosses 15th Street, lifting one claw at a time, slowly, like a Zen master. Like the doe. Green. Like the clean and gleaming surface of a dish or a window freshly washed.

THE END

Pages 10, 15, 97: Samuel Beckett quote "light gleams an instant" from *Waiting for Godot*.

Page 8: Arctic ground squirrel online image with permission from Canadian Museum of Nature, Ottawa, ON.

Page 22: Facts about arctic ground squirrels from the Internet Report from the New Hampshire Public Television, 268 Mast Road, Durham, NH 03824: WWW.NHPTV.ORG/NATUREWORKS/ARCTICGROUNDSQUIRREL.HTM and from

Arctic Ground Squirrel Report: BBC—Science and Nature, Wildfacts. WWW.BBC.CO.UK/NATURE/WILDFACTS/FACTFILES/3003.SHTML.

Page 23: The moon jellyfish image is public domain from NASA.

Page 25: Roy Rogers quotes from THINKEXIST.COM/QUOTES/ROY_ROGERS.

Page 29: Archaeopteryx quote from KQED and WWW/UCMP.BERKELEY.EDU/DIAPSIDS/BIRDS/ARCHEOPTERYX.

Page 37: Cat image found on public domain: OZELOTFELISPARDALIS.GIF, PHILOGRAPHIKON@T-ONLINE.DE.

Page 39: Facts about cats from MAXELLAH.TRIPOD.COM/CATFACTS; WWW.GEOCITIES.COM/SANDYTRACKER/CATFACTS.HTML; WWW.NATIONALGEOGRAPHIC.COM/CATS/SK1.HTML.

Page 45: quote from Locke from Webster's New Universal Unabridged Dictionary WWW.BRAINYQUOTE.COM/QUOTES/AUTHORS/J/JOHN_LOCKE.HTML.

Page 46: Facts about cotton: WWW.CCGGA.ORG/COTTON_INFORMATION/COTTON.HTML and personal communication.

Page 56: "Microscopic view of bug" photo online with permission from Ros

King: Natural History of England, by Benjamin Martin originally included within issues of The General Magazine of Arts and Sciences.

Page 59: Quote from The Handbook of Household Science (1879) by Edward L. Youmans, M.D., pg. 61, D. Appleton and Company, New York.

Page 62: Quote from An Outline of Psychoanalysis by Sigmund Freud, The James Strachey Translation, pg. 1, W.W. Norton and Company, New York and London.

Page 66: Facts about jellyfish from WWW.AQUATICCOMMUNITY.COM/JELLYFISH/FACTS.PHP; and WWW.DNR.SC.GOV/MARINE/PUB/SEASCIENCE/JELLYFI.HTML

Page 67: The archaeopteryx image found online in public domain from Arts and Sciences.

Page 87: Figure 1—A projection map compiled by P. Clay Sherrod, Arkansas Sky Observatory, from 378 visual drawings of Mars in the year 1971. WWW.ARKSKY.ORG/MARS2003.HTML.

The author thanks the public radio stations including KQED, KALW, and KPFA for their inspiring programs that remain part of her daily life.

FACTS ABOUT HUMANS

Every day 1.5 million people walk through Times Square in New York.

Every day almost as many people—1.5 million—board U.S. passenger planes.

The human eye blinks an average of 4,200,000 times a year.

The average person falls asleep in seven minutes.

The average person has 100,000 hairs on his/her head. Each hair grows about 5 inches (12.7 cm) every year.

Most people blink about 17,000 times a day.

Seventy percent of the dust in your home consists of shed human skin.

Only humans sleep on their backs.

There are more living organisms on the skin of a single human being than there are human beings on the surface of the earth.

NONA CASPERS lives in San Francisco with her partner, little dog Edgar, and cat Marie. She is an Associate Professor in the Creative Writing Program at San Francisco State University. Her book of stories *Heavier Than Air* (University of Massachusetts Press) won the Grace Paley Prize in Short Fiction and was a *New York Times Book Review* Editors' Choice. Her stories have been published in journals and anthologies such as the *Iowa Review, Ontario Review, Cimarron Review, Voyages Out 2 (Seal Press), Women on Women* (Plume), and the *Hers* series (Faber and Faber). Her work has been honored with a National Endowment for the Arts Fellowship, Iowa Review Fiction Award, Joseph Henry Jackson Literary Grant and Award, Barbara Deming Memorial Grant and Award and LAMBDA nomination. *Little Book of Days* started as a project to track her days, which she did for four hundred days. She teaches an MFA Dailiness course at San Francisco State University. www.nonacaspers.com

S P U Y T E N D U Y V I L

Meeting Eyes Bindery
Triton
Lithic Scatter

8TH AVENUE   Stefan Brecht

A DAY AND A NIGHT AT THE BATHS   Michael Rumaker

ACTS OF LEVITATION   Laynie Browne

ALIEN MATTER   Regina Derieva

ANARCHY   Mark Scroggins

APO/CALYPSO   Gordon Osing

APPLES OF THE EARTH   Dina Elenbogen

APPROXIMATING DIAPASON   hastain & thilleman

ARC: CLEAVAGE OF GHOSTS   Noam Mor

THE ARSENIC LOBSTER   Peter Grandbois

ASHES RAIN DOWN   William Luvaas

AUNTIE VARVARA'S CLIENTS   Stelian Tanase

BALKAN ROULETTE   Drazan Gunjaca

THE BANKS OF HUNGER AND HARDSHIP   J. Hunter Patterson

LA BELLE DAME   Gordon Osing & Tom Carlson

BIRD ON THE WING   Juana Culhane

BLACK LACE   Barbara Henning

BLACK MOUNTAIN DAYS   Michael Rumaker

BLUEPRINTS FOR A GENOCIDE   Rob Cook

BOTH SIDES OF THE NIGER   Andrew Kaufman

BREATHING FREE   (ed.) Vyt Bakaitis

Burial Ship   Nikki Stiller

Butterflies   Brane Mozetic

By The Time You Finish This Book

   You Might Be Dead   Aaron Zimmerman

Cadences   j/j hastain

Captivity Narratives   Richard Blevins

Celestial Monster   Juana Culhane

Cephalonical Sketches   t thilleman

Cleopatra Haunts the Hudson   Sarah White

Cloud Fire   Katherine Hastings

Columns: Track 2   Norman Finkelstein

Collected Poems of Lev Loseff   (ed.) Henry Pickford

Consciousness Suite   David Landrey

The Conviction & Subsequent

   Life of Savior Neck   Christian TeBordo

Conviction's Net of Branches   Michael Heller

The Corybantes   Tod Thilleman

Crossing Borders   Kowit & Silverberg

Day Book of a Virtual Poet   Robert Creeley

Daylight to Dirty Work   Tod Thilleman

The Desire Notebooks   John High

Detective Sentences   Barbara Henning

Diary of a Clone   Saviana Stanescu

Diffidence   Jean Harris

Donna Cameron   Donna Cameron

DON'T KILL ANYONE, I LOVE YOU   Gojmir Polajnar

DRAY-KHMARA AS A POET   Oxana Asher

EGGHEAD TO UNDERHOOF   Tod Thilleman

EROTICIZING THE NATION   Leverett T. Smith, Jr.

THE EVIL QUEEN   Benjamin Perez

EXILED FROM THE WOMB   Adrian Sangeorzan

EXTREME POSITIONS   Stephen Bett

THE FARCE   Carmen Firan

FISSION AMONG THE FANATICS   Tom Bradley

THE FLAME CHARTS   Paul Oppenheimer

FLYING IN WATER   Barbara Tomash

FORM   Martin Nakell

GESTURE THROUGH TIME   Elizabeth Block

GHOSTS!   Martine Bellen

GIRAFFES IN HIDING   Carol Novack

GNOSTIC FREQUENCIES   Patrick Pritchett

GOD'S WHISPER   Dennis Barone

GOWANUS CANAL, HANS KNUDSEN   Tod Thilleman

HALF-GIRL   Stephanie Dickinson

HIDDEN DEATH, HIDDEN ESCAPE   Liviu Georgescu

HOUNDSTOOTH   David Wirthlin

IDENTITY   Basil King

IN TIMES OF DANGER   Paul Oppenheimer

INCRETION   Brian Strang

INFERNO   Carmen Firan

INFINITY SUBSECTIONS   Mark DuCharme

INSOUCIANCE   Thomas Phillips

INVERTED CURVATURES   Francis Raven

THE IVORY HOUR   Laynie Browne

JACKPOT   Tsipi Keller

THE JAZZER & THE LOITERING LADY   Gordon Osing

KISSING NESTS   Werner Lutz, trans. by Marc Vincenz

KNOWLEDGE   Michael Heller

LADY V.   D.R. Popa

LAST SUPPER OF THE SENSES   Dean Kostos

A LESSER DAY   Andrea Scrima

LET'S TALK ABOUT DEATH   M. Maurice Abitbol

LIBRETTO FOR THE EXHAUSTED WORLD   Michael Fisher

LIGHT HOUSE   Brian Lucas

LIGHT YEARS: MULTIMEDIA IN THE
EAST VILLAGE, 1960-1966   (ed.) Carol Bergé

LITTLE BOOK OF DAYS   Nona Caspers

LITTLE TALES OF FAMILY & WAR   Martha King

LONG FALL: ESSAYS AND TEXTS   Andrey Gritsman

LUNACIES   Ruxandra Cesereanu

LUST SERIES   Stephanie Dickinson

LYRICAL INTERFERENCE   Norman Finkelstein

MAINE BOOK   Joe Cardarelli (ed.) Anselm Hollo

MANNHATTeN   Sarah Rosenthal

MATING IN CAPTIVITY   Nava Renek

MEANWHILE   Gordon Osing

MEDIEVAL OHIO   Richard Blevins

MEMORY'S WAKE   Derek Owens

MERMAID'S PURSE   Laynie Browne

MIMING MINK   j/j hastain

MOBILITY LOUNGE   David Lincoln

MODERN ADVENTURES   Bill Evans

THE MOSCOVIAD   Yuri Andrukhovych

MULTIFESTO: A HENRI D'MESCAN READER   Davis Schneiderman

MY LAST CENTURY   Joanna Sit

THE NEW BEAUTIFUL TENDONS   Jeffery Beam

NIGHTSHIFT / AN AREA OF SHADOWS   Erika Burkart & Ernst Halter

NO PERFECT WORDS   Nava Renek

NO WRONG NOTES   Norman Weinstein

NORTH & SOUTH   Martha King

NOTES OF A NUDE MODEL   Harriet Sohmers Zwerling

THE NUMBER OF MISSING   Adam Berlin

OF ALL THE CORNERS TO FORGET   Gian Lombardo

ONÖNYXA & THERSEYN   T Thilleman

THE OPENING DAY   Richard Blevins

OUR FATHER   M.G. Stephens

OVER THE LIFELINE   Adrian Sangeorzan

PAGAN DAYS   Michael Rumaker

PART OF THE DESIGN   Laura E. Wright

PIECES FOR SMALL ORCHESTRA & OTHER FICTIONS   Norman Lock

A PLACE IN THE SUN   Lewis Warsh

THE POET : PENCIL PORTRAITS   Basil King

POLITICAL ECOSYSTEMS   J.P. Harpignies

POWERS: TRACK 3   Norman Finkelstein

THE PRISON NOTEBOOKS OF ALAN KRIEGER (TERRORIST)   Marc Estrin

THE PROPAGANDA FACTORY   Marc Vincenz

PSYCHONAUTICA   Paul Doru

COLUMNS: TRACK 2   Norman Finkelstein

REMAINS TO BE SEEN   Halvard Johnson

RETELLING   Tsipi Keller

RIVERING   Dean Kostos

ROOT-CELLAR TO RIVERINE   Tod Thilleman

THE ROOTS OF HUMAN SEXUALITY   M. Maurice Abitbol

SAIGON AND OTHER POEMS   Jack Walters

A SARDINE ON VACATION   Robert Castle

SAVOIR FEAR   Charles Borkhuis

SECRET OF WHITE   Barbara Tomash

SEDUCTION   Lynda Schor

SEE WHAT YOU THINK   David Rosenberg

SETTLEMENT   Martin Nakell

SEX AND THE SENIOR CITY   M. Maurice Abitbol

SKETCHES IN NORSE & FORRA   t thilleman

SKETCHES TZITZIMIME   t thilleman

SLAUGHTERING THE BUDDHA   Gordon Osing

THE SNAIL'S SONG   Alta Ifland

SOS: SONG OF SONGS OF SOLOMON   j/j hastain

THE SPARK SINGER   Jade Sylvan

SPIRITLAND   Nava Renek

STRANGE EVOLUTIONARY FLOWERS   Lizbeth Rymland

SUDDENLY TODAY WE CAN DREAM   Rutha Rosen

THE SUDDEN DEATH OF...   Serge Gavronsky

THE TAKEAWAY BIN   Toni Mirosevich

THE TATTERED LION   Juana Culhane

TAUTOLOGICAL EYE   Martin Nakell

TED'S FAVORITE SKIRT   Lewis Warsh

THEATER OF SKIN   Gordon Osing & Tom Carlson

THINGS THAT NEVER HAPPENED   Gordon Osing

THREAD   Vasyl Makhno

THREE MOUTHS   Tod Thilleman

THREE SEA MONSTERS   Tod Thilleman

TRACK   Norman Finkelstein

TRANSITORY   Jane Augustine

TRANSPARENCIES LIFTED FROM NOON   Chris Glomski

TRIPLE CROWN SONNETS   Jeffrey Cyphers Wright

TSIM-TSUM   Marc Estrin

TWELVE CIRCLES   Yuri Andrukhovych

VIENNA ØØ   Eugene K. Garber

UNCENSORED SONGS FOR SAM ABRAMS   (ed.) John Roche

UP FISH CREEK ROAD   David Matlin

WARP SPASM   Basil King

WATCHFULNESS   Peter O'Leary

WATCH THE DOORS AS THEY CLOSE   Karen Lillis

WALKING AFTER MIDNIGHT   Bill Kushner

WEST OF WEST END   Peter Freund

WHEN THE GODS COME HOME TO ROOST   Marc Estrin

WHIRLIGIG   Christopher Salerno

WHITE, CHRISTIAN   Christopher Stoddard

WINTER LETTERS   Vasyl Makhno

WITHIN THE SPACE BETWEEN   Stacy Cartledge

A WORLD OF NOTHING BUT NATIONS   Tod Thilleman

A WORLD OF NOTHING BUT SELF-INFLICTION   Tod Thilleman

WRECKAGE OF REASON   (ed.) Nava Renek

XIAN DYAD   Jason Price Everett

The YELLOW HOUSE   Robin Behn

YOU, ME, AND THE INSECTS   Barbara Henning

Made in the USA
San Bernardino, CA
29 January 2019